A
Little Red Truck
Mystery

Rick Ellinger

Thanks and praise to the Lord,
for the inspiration and ideas.

Thanks to my wife, Ruby,
for her editing and encouragement.

Thanks to all of my little red truck friends.

Chapter 1 - Trouble and Plan

It was still early in the fall, and the foliage colors were still quite vibrant. But, some of the leaves were beginning to fall to the ground as the winter season approached.

Chuck enjoyed this time of year. It was still warm, but not the intense heat of summer. He had the windows rolled down as he drove his restored, red truck down the country road toward Jackie's house.

Jackie and Chuck had been casually dating for a few weeks, ever since their first ride together in Chuck's newly restored vintage pickup truck. It was nothing too serious. Neither of them really even claimed it was "dating".

On this warm, fall Sunday morning, Chuck was to pick Jackie up at her house outside of town. As he approached her house and saw her standing outside waiting for him, Chuck remembered that first time she had ridden in his truck, after it had been restored. That was the day he had met Jackie.

Chuck parked the truck, got out and walked around to the passenger side. "Good morning," Chuck said as he opened the door for her.

"Good morning," she replied. She climbed in, and he closed the door.

As they rode toward the church, Jackie said, "I still can't get over how nice your truck looks now. It's too bad it can't be seen by more people, especially my red truck friends."

"You posted photos online for all of your red truck friends, didn't you?" Chuck asked, pretty sure of the answer.

"Yes," she replied, "but that's just not the same. "To see it up close and in person is different."

"Yes," Chuck agreed, "I guess I see what you mean. What do you do in those red truck social groups anyway?"

"We share photos of our collections and of all the ways we use our trucks in our homes," Jackie began. "We also show all of our red truck purchases and home decor items. We like to see what others find and how they use them for each season. Some people actually do crafts with their truck items and sell them online and at craft shows."

"Cool," Chuck said. "Sounds like fun."

"And," Jackie continued, "when we find a beautiful old truck sitting somewhere, like this one, we like to share photos of our discoveries."

"Maybe I should sell photos of my truck," Chuck suggested with a grin that indicated he was really only joking.

"That wouldn't be a bad idea, actually," Jackie said as they pulled into the church parking lot. "There would be people who would buy them. They might even use them on greeting cards and other crafts."

Later that morning, after the church service, Chuck and Jackie were talking to Pastor Randall and his wife, Martha.

A woman approached them that Chuck had seen before, but he did not know who she was. She always seemed to be dressed very sharply and business-like.

"Good morning, Pastor Randall," the woman said as she shook the pastor's hand. "And, good morning Martha."

"Good morning, Susan," they both responded simultaneously.

"Susan, I don't think you have met
Chuck Mainor," Pastor Randall said as he
motioned toward his two friends standing
nearby.

"Chuck, this is Susan Wellers, our town
mayor and member of our church," the pastor
continued. "Jackie, I believe you have
already met her."

"Yes, good to see you this morning,"
Jackie said as she shook Susan's hand.

"Good to meet you," Chuck added. He
extended his hand as well.

"It is nice to meet you too, Chuck," the
mayor said as she shook his hand. "Do you
live in town?"

"Yes, just on the other side," he replied.

"Always glad to meet a local," the
mayor said warmly and with a friendly smile.

Susan turned toward Pastor Randall,
"I'm sorry to interrupt you folks, but I needed
to talk to you before we leave here this
morning. It won't take but a moment."

"No problem at all," the pastor replied.

"We will get going and let you all talk," Jackie offered.

"No," the mayor said quickly. "I would not mind if you stayed. Actually, I would like for you to hear what I have to say, also."

"What's on your mind, Susan?" the pastor asked.

"I need for you all to pray," Susan shared.

"Of course," Pastor Randall said. "What's going on?"

"It's our town," she began to explain. "It's in trouble financially. Businesses are threatening to leave. The large manufacturing plant on the edge of town is considering relocating. That will, of course, mean many lost jobs, or people leaving town to keep their job at the new location. We need new business. We need a way to stimulate the local economy."

She paused before continuing. "Our

town has been declining for quite a while, since before my administration. But, of course, many on the town council want to blame it on me. I am mayor now, so it is my responsibility in a way.”

“It is hardly your fault,” Martha stated while shaking her head in disbelief. “You have been the best mayor this town has had in years.”

“Thank you, Martha,” Susan said humbly. “Unfortunately, not everyone agrees with that sentiment. We will have more discussions at our upcoming town council meetings. I just wanted to ask for your prayers.”

“We will all certainly be praying about it,” Pastor Randall stated very positively.

Everyone else also expressed their agreement to do so.

“Why don’t we pray together now?” Martha suggested.

“Great idea!” Pastor Randall said as he

bowed his head and closed his eyes.

The others did the same as Pastor Randall began to pray. "Dear Lord, You alone are our Creator and our God. You alone are on the throne and are worthy of all praise and glory. You are in control, and we acknowledge Your sovereign power. We ask for Your help in the request that our mayor, our friend, our sister has brought before us. We ask that You would give wisdom to her and to our town council. Help them to each see clearly what needs to be done to help our beloved town. We ask, not because we are worthy or deserving, but because You are merciful and loving. Please show the way. We ask in Jesus' mighty name. Amen."

The others echoed with, "Amen."

"Thank you, Pastor Randall," Susan said as she dabbed her watery eyes with a tissue.

"As we were praying, I got an idea," Jackie shared excitedly. "Maybe a big event is what we need to have. Something that would attract lots of outside vendors and visitors." She then paused for a moment.

"I know it might sound crazy, but, what about a Little Red Truck Christmas Festival?

"You and your little red trucks," Chuck said jokingly and laughed as he thought about her vast collection of the vintage automobiles inside and outside her home.

They all laughed.

"I love the idea!" Martha said with a huge smile on her face.

"You would," her husband also joked.

Everyone laughed again, knowing her collection almost rivaled Jackie's.

They all seemed to be pondering the idea, waiting for someone else to speak.

"That might actually be a good idea," Chuck said, breaking the silence.

"Yes," Jackie continued with her idea, "with the popularity of red trucks across the country, we could bring in people from all over."

"That really doesn't sound crazy to me at all," Susan finally spoke up. "And, there is no Christmas festival anywhere near here that I am aware of."

"It could possibly bring in vendors as well as collectors from all over the country," Jackie continued. "And, it would bring in lots of business for local stores and hotels."

"It would cost up front though, for promotion, set up, etcetera," Susan said.

"And, a whole lot of time and work," Chuck added.

"We could charge the vendors for their space," Jackie suggested. "That would help offset some of the initial costs."

"I love it," Susan said. "And, the town would receive the local taxes on all of the transactions."

"It would bring in lots of business to local restaurants and hotels, plus, gas stations and more," Chuck added.

"We can ask the local businesses to contribute funds and decorations," Martha said, "and anything else that is needed. Since we will hopefully be bringing in business to town, it will help them all."

"Yes," Jackie agreed.

"We can also ask the hotels to give special rates to festival vendors," Pastor Randall added. "Are you thinking it would be a three day event, for a weekend?"

"Yes," Jackie replied. "That is kind of what I was thinking. What do you all think?"

"Sounds like a good idea," Susan agreed. "And what about having it on the first or second weekend of December? Giving people time to do some Christmas shopping and still be close to Christmas."

Everyone was in agreement, and their excitement grew.

"We only have a few months to pull it off," Pastor Randall reminded them. "Less than three actually."

"We can do it if we all work together," Jackie stated confidently. "And, with the Lord's help, of course."

"Let's do it!" Susan almost shouted.

"Count us in," Pastor Randall offered. "Just let us know what we can do to help."

"We need to get together and begin planning and making contacts," Susan said.

"We can meet at our house," Martha offered.

"That would be great," Jackie responded. "Thank you!"

"We have a home group meeting tomorrow, night," Martha continued. "How about we meet Tuesday night at 6:00? Does that suit everyone?"

"Suits me," Chuck agreed.

"Me too!" Jackie said.

"Me too!" Susan added. "This will be so great!"

"We will be the First Annual Little Red Truck Festival Committee," Chuck said with joyful enthusiasm.

"That sounds awesome!" Jackie almost shouted her words in her excitement.

"And, let's be sure to continue praying," Chuck suggested.

"Yes," Pastor Randall agreed, "for sure!"

"Thank you all so very much," Susan said. "I truly mean it. My prayer has already been answered, more than I could have expected."

Chapter 2 - Secret Revealed

After taking Jackie home, Chuck spent that afternoon researching online. He wanted to look for ideas for festivals. He typed "red truck festivals" in the search bar on his web browser and clicked on the search button.

"Wow," he said out loud as the results appeared on his screen. "That is very interesting." He tried a few other searches. "Cool, I can't wait to tell Jackie."

When Jackie arrived later that evening, He told her about his findings. "You will never guess what I found out."

"What's that?" she asked.

"I searched online for red truck festivals, just to look for ideas and to see what had been done by others."

"Great idea," Jackie said.

"I could find no evidence that a red truck festival has ever been done before," Chuck continued.

"Seriously? Wow!" Jackie exclaimed with even more excitement than she had displayed earlier in presenting the initial idea.

"So, ours will be the first?"

"It looks like it," Chuck replied.

"That is so cool!" Jackie exclaimed.

"That makes the whole thing even more exciting!"

"I thought you might like to hear that."

"I have also been thinking a lot about it all afternoon," Jackie said, "and I came up with the perfect idea for the main setting and display."

"Tell me. I'm all ears."

"Picture this," Jackie began. "We put your newly restored red truck and my unrestored truck in front of that stone wall in the town square. They will be facing each other." She used her hands to describe the position of the trucks relative to one another.

"We can put a large Christmas tree in the center just behind the two trucks, and maybe string some Christmas lights across the wall."

"That's a cool idea," Chuck responded. "It would make a great photo opportunity for everyone coming to the festival."

"Exactly!" Jackie said.

"We could even charge for the photos," Chuck added.

"I had thought about that too, but would probably like to keep it free. All of the vendors will be charging for their items, and everyone will have to pay for travel, lodging and all, so we can offer this to them for free.

Besides, people will take photos with their own smartphones anyway, so it would be hard to control it."

"True, good points," Chuck said. "I fully agree with you. Sorry, I'm always thinking like an accountant."

They both laughed.

"I would like to get my truck all cleaned up and make it more presentable," Jackie continued, "even if it is all rusty. I don't want to get it fully restored but just fixed up a bit. I still want it to look like an old, vintage truck. Does that make sense?"

"Yes, it makes perfect sense," Chuck acknowledged. "And I would be glad to help you."

"Thank you, Chuck. Can we work on it in your shop? I hate to impose and take up room in your garage, but the weather is getting colder and working on it outside might be challenging at best."

"Of course we can," Chuck replied.

"Great idea, actually, especially since I have all the tools there and everything. And, there is plenty of space too, so it won't be any problem at all."

"Thank you," Jackie said with a big smile as she leaned toward him and gently hugged him.

"We will need to haul your truck to my shop on my trailer," Chuck added, "since yours doesn't have a fuel pump to run." He realized his mistake as soon as the words came out of his mouth.

"How do you know it doesn't have a fuel pump?" Jackie asked. She did not sound upset. Chuck was glad of that. But, she did sound rather surprised.

"I'm sorry," Chuck replied rather hesitantly. "I was supposed to keep that a secret. I know you didn't want it revealed that the pump came from you."

"Wait a minute. Pastor Randall actually told you?" She sounded a little more irritated now.

"It wasn't his fault," Chuck explained. "I actually guessed it. He asked me not to say anything, so I hadn't all this time. I tried to honor your desire to keep it a secret." He paused in thought for a moment. "But, I really did want to thank you," he added.

"It's okay," she said. "I don't mind that you know. I'm actually glad. It's sort of a relief to not have to hide the secret anymore."

"I agree," Chuck stated. "So, now that it is in the open, thank you." He hugged her as he said, "Thank you very much. That was really kind and generous of you."

"You're quite welcome," she replied as she returned his embrace.

Chapter 3 - Discovery

The following evening, Chuck drove his truck over to Jackie's. This time, he was pulling his flatbed trailer behind it. The trailer was also red, which matched his truck perfectly.

When he arrived at her house, he backed the trailer up to her old truck, taking care, as much as possible, to not mess up her grass. He was really glad the soil was a little hard and not wet. That would help to keep the weight of the trucks from making deep impressions in the yard.

Jackie's old, unrestored truck looked to be in fairly good shape. Chuck had seen it before, but had not really gotten that close. It was in much better shape than his had been in before the restoration. The faded color still revealed its original red tint, and it was not nearly as rusty as Chuck's had been.

The back of the truck was filled with pumpkins that were sitting on wooden crates. And, there were fall wreaths and foliage all around the exterior of the bed. Obviously, this was Jackie's display for the fall season.

Jackie met him just as he was getting out of his truck.

"Hi, Chuck," she greeted him with a warm smile. "Nice evening for this. Isn't it?"

"Hi, Jackie. Yes, it certainly is."

Chuck walked closer to her truck and added, "Your fall display looks nice."

"Thanks," Jackie said. "I change the items in the back of the truck for each season.”

Jackie watched as Chuck knelt down to inspect one of the front tires.

“Is everything okay with the tire?” Jackie asked.

“Yes,” he answered as he moved to the other front tire. “I was checking to make sure they have enough air pressure to roll up onto the trailer. I brought my air compressor just in case. They seem to be in fine shape.”

“I was wondering something,” Jackie said and then paused.

“What’s that?” Chuck asked.

“How are we going to get my truck onto the trailer? Since it won’t run, we can’t drive it on there. I guess I should have thought of that before now.” She laughed at herself.

“I brought my winch and chain,” Chuck began to explain. “That will pull it right up onto the trailer. No problem.”

He paused before adding, “Hopefully.”

"Awesome!" Jackie responded. "I knew you would have it all worked out. So, what can I do to help?"

"Well, let's take the crates and pumpkins out of the bed and all of the decorations off the outside. Then, we will get the chain hooked up and let the winch do the work."

"Okay, good idea," Jackie said as she grabbed a pumpkin from the back of her truck. "I should have already done that. I never thought about it."

"No problem," Chuck replied as he also removed a pumpkin from one of the crates.

Chuck was about to remove a wreath from the exterior of the bed when he said, "Oh my goodness! That's funny!"

"What is?" Jackie asked as she looked up from her work on the other side of the truck.

"You're going to think I am totally crazy," Chuck said. "But, I did not realize your truck was a flatbed and dually. With all of the decorations on it, I had just never noticed. I assumed it was a regular pickup like mine."

He looked more closely and examined the side rails on both sides of the bed. They each consisted of two wooden planks that ran the entire length of the bed and came up half the height of the cab.

Each wheel had exposed lug nuts, where his truck had small, chrome hub caps covering the center portion. And, the rear axle had two tires on each side, allowing for the extra weight of a larger payload in the bed.

"Will that be a problem?" Jackie asked. "That mine is a flatbed, I mean?"

"Oh, no," Chuck replied quickly. "That's not a problem at all. I just can't believe I never noticed that."

"I'm kind of surprised too, that you never did."

They both laughed.

"We can remove the side rails if you think that would be better for the display," Jackie suggested.

"We should probably leave them on there," Chuck suggested as he looked more closely at them. "They add a lot to the character of the truck. Plus, they might help to discourage anyone from climbing up onto the bed for photos."

"Excellent point," Jackie agreed.

"And, they are in really great shape," Chuck added.

"Ok, good," Jackie said cheerfully. "Oh, by the way, I don't think you're crazy. Not *totally*, at least."

They both laughed again.

"Your grandfather must have been a farmer to have owned a truck like this," Chuck said.

"That's the funny thing," Jackie responded. "He wasn't a farmer. But, I do remember that this truck came in handy many times when his friends needed things moved or hauled from place to place."

"Maybe that's why he bought it," Chuck suggested, "just to help people."

"Could be," Jackie said. "He was like that. Always wanting to be a help to someone if he could."

After they had finished removing all of the decorations, they hooked one end of a chain to the frame of Chuck's truck and the other end to the winch. Then, they hooked another chain to the frame of Jackie's truck and to the other side of the winch.

"Okay, here we go," Chuck stated. "Stand clear."

Jackie stepped back, and Chuck powered on the winch. The chain jerked and her truck barely moved.

"What's wrong?" Jackie asked. "It's not moving."

"Oops," Chuck said as he powered off

the winch. "I guess we had better release the brake in your truck and take it out of gear."

"I can do that," Jackie acknowledged as she walked over to her truck and opened the door. She climbed in and released the brake lever and then moved the shifter into neutral.

As she climbed back out of her truck, Jackie said, "Okay, give it another try."

Chuck powered on the winch again, and this time, Jackie's truck lurched forward slightly as its tires broke free from their resting place in the yard. Then, it started rolling freely. It ascended the ramps to the trailer with no problem.

Once they had it securely in place and chained to the trailer, they both climbed into Chuck's truck and proceeded down the road toward his house.

"This is quite the picture," Chuck said as he glanced in his rearview mirror. "A restored truck hauling an unrestored truck. It reminds me of the Bible verse I just read in my devotions the other day that says we should carry each other's burdens."

"Yes, great point," Jackie replied. "That verse also says when we do carry each other's burdens, we fulfill the law of Christ. I think that verse is Galatians 6:2, isn't it?"

"Yes, it is," Chuck acknowledged. "Very good!"

"And, speaking of filling," Chuck said, grinning at his clever transition, "I know you don't want to fully restore your truck, but I was wondering if you would like for me to fill the holes in its body and spray base primer on any bare metal spots. That wouldn't really change the overall appearance much, and it would help to keep the rust from getting any worse."

"Yes, that would be nice," Jackie agreed. "If it is not too much trouble."

"No trouble at all," Chuck replied. "I would be glad to do that for you."

"Thank you," Jackie said as she smiled

and placed her hand gently on his arm.

"You're quite welcome."

When they arrived at Chuck's house, he backed the trailer up to the garage. As they unchained her truck, Jackie said, "I was thinking, for our display, I would love to be able to hang a Christmas wreath on the door of each of our trucks."

"That would make a great addition to the scene and for the photos," Chuck said.

"Yes," Jackie continued, "but, how can we attach them without damaging the trucks and without having a string or ribbon or something hanging down to hold them?"

"Maybe magnets would work," Chuck suggested. "We could attach them to the backs of the wreaths and just hang them on the truck doors."

"Great idea!" Jackie responded. "I think that would work!"

"Now," Chuck said, "if you will get into your truck and control the steering and the brakes, I think I can push it off of the trailer."

"Okay, will do!" Jackie replied as she climbed up onto the trailer and into her truck.

They rolled her truck off of the trailer and into place in the bay of Chuck's garage where he had previously done the restoration work on his own truck. It was all rather symbolic, Chuck thought, since her truck had been the donor of the needed fuel pump.

"I was wondering something," Chuck said as he headed over to his workbench. "Before you gave your fuel pump to me, was there anything wrong with your truck's engine that would have caused it not to run?"

"I was told it had a cracked block or something," Jackie answered. "It was going to cost thousands to repair and then even more to restore. I really didn't care to spend that much since I wanted to leave it in its vintage look anyway."

"Oh, okay," Chuck said as he nodded

his head. "I just wondered."

Jackie began to work on cleaning her truck while Chuck sanded some rough areas and filled some holes in its body and fenders.

"So, tell me something," Chuck said as he continued to work. "I don't think you ever told me. What got you into collecting little red trucks, anyway?"

Jackie grinned and laughed slightly. "Now you're going to think *I'm* the crazy one."

"No, I won't," Chuck replied. "I promise."

"It was mainly because of this truck, actually," she began to explain. "When my grandfather left it to me, I almost sold it. Since it was the only thing I had of his, I decided to keep it. Plus, I remember when I used to ride in it with him into town and places." She paused while thinking of the memories. "Those are good memories. I think that might be why he left it to me."

"Then," she continued, "I began to notice the red truck items everywhere. I had never paid any attention to them before, so I never really noticed. But, they began popping up all over and in just about every store."

"Once something is on your mind like that," Chuck stated, "you begin to notice it around you more."

"Yes, that is so true," Jackie continued. "And, like I said, they were everywhere. Each one that I saw reminded me more and more of this truck and of my grandfather. So, I finally bought one that I liked. Once I bought that first one, I was hooked on them from then on."

They both laughed.

"I'm going to work on cleaning the inside a little," Jackie said as she opened the passenger door of her truck. "In case anyone looks inside, I want it to be presentable."

"Good idea," Chuck replied.

"I haven't really looked in here too

much," she said as she leaned inside. "It's just been sitting out in the yard collecting dust."

"And rust," Chuck added with a laugh.

"Yes, that too." Jackie also laughed. "I'm actually glad we are going to prevent some of that. Thank you for your help."

"You're quite welcome. I'm glad to do it."

"The glove box seems to be jammed," Jackie said. "I can't get it opened."

"Let me take a look," Chuck said as he came around to the passenger side and looked inside. He pressed the button on the box and nothing happened. "The catch seems to be stuck. Let me try something."

He walked over to his workbench and took a screwdriver from the pegboard.

"I have never even tried to open it before," Jackie said as he returned with his screwdriver.

"Let's see if we can get this to work

without damaging it," he said as he stuck the flat end of the screwdriver into the top of the glove box where the latch was connected.

The glove box popped open.

"There you go!" Chuck said with a grin.

"Great! Thank you! You are quite handy to have around."

"Sometimes," he replied with a sly grin.

Chuck returned to filling holes in the body while Jackie began to clean out the glove box contents.

"Wow," Jackie exclaimed, "he must have not thrown anything away. There are gas receipts in here for a long way back. And, there are also lots of the old vehicle registrations where he renewed it each year and kept the old ones."

She pulled out papers and receipts and piled them beside her on the seat.

The box was nearly empty when she found a piece of paper wedged in the back. She pulled on it, but it was stuck. She pulled a little harder, and the paper ripped. She removed the piece that was now free and in her hand and read it to herself.

"I found something interesting in here," Jackie said as she climbed out of the truck and walked toward Chuck.

"What is it?" Chuck asked.

"It looks like a very old vehicle registration. It's not as detailed as the more modern ones. The date on it is 1953."

"Interesting," Chuck said. "That should be about the year this truck was manufactured and first sold. That is probably the first time it was registered to the original owner."

"True," Jackie agreed. "And, the really interesting thing is that the name on this registration is not my grandfather's like on all the others I found in there."

"What is the name?" Chuck asked.

"Only the last name is showing," Jackie answered. "It is Miller. The first name was ripped off and is probably on the piece that is still stuck down in the back of the glove box."

"That was probably the first owner of the truck," Chuck said. "He must have bought it when it was brand new."

"Yes, that could be" Jackie agreed. "But, I don't recognize the name. My grandfather left the truck to me in his will, and I just assumed he was the original and only owner. So, I don't know who owned it before he did."

"Apparently a Mister or Miss Miller," Chuck said with a sly grin.

"I say!" Jackie exclaimed in a fake British accent. "I do believe you are right, Sherlock!"

They both laughed.

"Can I see it?" Chuck said as he reached for the registration paper.

Jackie handed it to him, and he studied it for a moment. "The address is here in town, but I don't remember any residential houses that far out on that road."

"Isn't that out where the manufacturing plant is located?" Jackie asked.

"Yes, and a Christmas tree farm across from it. But, that is all there is out that way, I think." Chuck then switched to his own version of a British accent. "I do believe we have a mystery on our hands, Miss Watson."

They both laughed again.

"I think you are right," Jackie replied. "Can we drive out there while we still have a little daylight and take a look?" Jackie asked.

"Sure, let's go!" Chuck answered with excitement in his voice. "We can take my truck."

They both climbed into his truck, and he started the engine.

"I'll bring up the address on my Global Map App," Jackie offered as she pulled her phone from the back pocket of her jeans. "At least that might get us close."

"Great idea," Chuck agreed as he shifted his truck into gear, and they proceeded down the road.

"The address doesn't show on the map as a valid address," Jackie said.

"Well, let's just see what is out that way," Chuck suggested. "Maybe we can figure it out."

They rode on for a little longer and turned onto the road that led out of town.

"This is the road on the registration," Chuck stated. "And there is the manufacturing plant on the left and the tree farm on the right."

Chuck slowed the truck down and announced, "The main entrance of the plant is down the road a little farther."

"Even though my map app doesn't show this specific address," Jackie said, "it should be right around here, based on the address of the plant and the farm. But, there is nothing else here. Very mysterious."

"It really does look like we have a mystery on our hands, Watson" Chuck said.

Jackie burst out laughing.

"What is it?" Chuck asked. "I didn't use my pathetic British accent that time."

"No," Jackie answered, "it's not that. I always liked reading mystery novels ever since I was a little girl. I have always wanted to solve a mystery. And now, it looks like I have that chance."

"Well, it doesn't look like we will get much further," Chuck said. "We might have hit a dead end in this mystery already."

"That is the way a good mystery always looks near the beginning," Jackie replied. "Or it wouldn't be a mystery."

"I guess you have a point there," Chuck agreed as he shifted his truck into second gear and increased the speed. "The plant goes all the way to the end of this road, so I'll turn around in their entranceway."

He pulled the truck into the plant's entrance and backed onto the road. Then, he shifted into first gear and headed in the direction from where they had just come.

They had driven only a very short distance when Jackie shouted, "Wait! Stop the truck! I think I saw something!"

"What was it? A dead body?" Chuck kidded as he stopped the truck. "Now you're beginning to imagine things."

"No, I don't mean anything like that," Jackie said as she opened the door and jumped out of the truck.

Chuck set the brake and got out of the truck. He followed Jackie down the road a short distance to a spot they had just passed.

Jackie began digging in the grass and weeds on the shoulder of the road with her hands.

"What in the world are you looking for?" Chuck asked.

"This!" she exclaimed as she moved a mound of dirt.

Jackie pointed to the edge of the road, and Chuck realized she had partially uncovered the remains of an old, concrete entranceway.

"They must have moved the entrance of the factory at some point," Chuck suggested.

"Then, why doesn't the address show as the plant's address?" Jackie asked. "It is actually several numbers off. It seems to be all one piece of property, so it should be one address."

"Yes, good point," Chuck replied. "I don't know, but this is about where the address should be according to the other numbers up and down the street."

"Now, I am really curious," Jackie stated. "I want to check into this some more."

"It would be interesting to find out who the man was and how your grandfather came to own the truck. I would also like to find out why this address changed. I'll help you, if you want."

"I would appreciate that a lot," Jackie replied. "Thank you. This is so exciting!"

Chapter 4 - Work Continues

When Tuesday night rolled around, the self-appointed festival committee gathered at Pastor Randall and Martha's house. Martha had prepared coffee and snacks, and everyone gathered in the dining room around the large family table.

"Thank you all for coming," Pastor Randall said to kick things off. "I am certainly not in charge here as this is more Jackie and Susan's event, but how about I start us out in prayer?"

"Yes, great idea," Jackie agreed. "Please do."

"Let's pray," Pastor Randall said as he bowed his head.

"Dear Heavenly Father, our Creator, our Redeemer, we love You, and we seek to do only Your will in all things. We need Your guidance in this endeavor and humbly ask for Your wisdom to direct our every decision, plan and action. We ask for Your blessing to make this festival a success for all involved. This evening, help us to begin the planning process. Help us to cover all the bases and accomplish what needs to be done. Help us to use our time productively and effectively. Most of all, let Your will be done. We thank You and ask these things in the precious name of Jesus. Amen!"

An echo of amens resounded around the table.

"Well, Jackie and Susan, what do we need to do first?" Pastor Randall asked.

"I'm probably not the one who should take the lead here. That position should go to our mayor," Jackie suggested as she looked toward Susan and grinned.

"No, not at all," Susan replied. "It was your idea, and I think you would make a great leader for our committee. All in favor say 'I'."

Everyone, except Jackie, said "I" in unison.

"I sense a conspiracy here," Jackie said with a laugh. "Susan, how about you and I co-lead? Can we do that?"

"Okay," Susan answered. "Agreed."

"Great!" Jackie stated. "Thank you, Susan. I did have some thoughts about what we might need to do to help us get started."

"Awesome!" Chuck said. "Let's hear them!"

"I think we need to search online, and maybe some other sources, and make a list of possible vendors to contact," Jackie explained.

"Yes, great idea," Susan said. "Maybe we should assign someone to start making that list. We can all add to it as we go."

"I could help with starting the list," Martha offered. "I can start right now on my tablet."

"Thank you, Martha," Susan said. "That would be great!"

"Let me ask everyone a question first," Martha said. "What type of vendors are we looking for? I mean, what types of things do we want them to sell, or what types of services do we want them to make available?"

"Very good question," Susan answered. "We certainly don't want to add any extra competition to our town's local stores and restaurants."

"Excellent point," Chuck replied. "Our goal is to help them, not to drive them out of business. And, we certainly want to be selective as to what we allow and what we don't allow."

"Yes, my thoughts exactly," Jackie interjected. "We certainly want this to be a family-friendly event. I was thinking that most of our vendors should be more home-made craft type things. But, not necessarily red trucks only. Any country type craft would be good. Especially Christmas items since it is a Christmas festival. Home decor and other items."

"Okay, great," Martha said. "That will give me a good place to start searching."

"I can add to the list also," Jackie continued. "A lot of my online social media friends are crafters. I am sure some of them would love to participate. It will give them a chance to build their businesses as well."

"Awesome!" Susan exclaimed.

"Martha, I'll make a list of those later and give it to you," Jackie added.

"Okay, thanks," Martha said as she made a note reminding herself to get that list from Jackie.

"And, speaking of helping our local stores and restaurants," Jackie continued, "I had an idea that might help to direct more traffic into their doors on the weekend of the festival. I saw in several Christmas movies last year where the towns had scavenger hunts. They were lots of fun for everyone."

"That does sound like fun," Susan said, "but, how would that help the local stores and businesses?"

"Oh, I think I get it," Martha jumped in. "We can put an item to be found in each of the stores and shops."

"Exactly!" Jackie confirmed.

"That's a great idea!" Pastor Randall exclaimed. "And, maybe some of those stores would be willing to offer prizes for the winners. That would also help to give them some added publicity."

"Yes!" Jackie agreed.

"I also have a suggestion," Chuck said.

"Let's hear it!" Jackie stated enthusiastically.

"I know the church building is a little outside of town," Chuck began, "but, what about having a presence at the festival for the church? We can use it as a ministry opportunity."

"That would be great!" Pastor Randall agreed with excitement in his voice. "I was sort of thinking along the same lines myself. I'm just not sure what we could do. I'll have to give that some thought and prayer."

"What about having the youth of the church present a Christmas story drama?" It was Martha who had offered the suggestion.

"Wow," Pastor Randall responded, "that would be fantastic!"

"I would be willing to direct them," Martha continued. "If you will help." She was looking at her husband when she made that last comment.

"I would be glad to," Pastor Randall

replied.

"We could hand out candy J's too!" Cheryl bounded in the room as she excitedly shared her suggestion.

"Someone has been listening from the next room," Martha said as she lifted her daughter to her lap.

"Candy J's?" Chuck asked.

"Candy canes turned upside down to form the letter J, for Jesus," Martha answered.

"Oh, that's cool!" Chuck responded.

"There is a legend that the candy cane was first designed as a J," Pastor Randall began to explain. "The stripes represent the blood that Jesus shed. The three small stripes are for the scars from the three nails. The large stripe is for the blood that flowed from His side when it was pierced by the Roman soldier's spear."

"I don't think I have ever heard about that before," Chuck said. "That is very powerful."

"We could hand out cards with that story on them," Cheryl added to her suggestion, "with the candy J's".

"Wonderful idea, Hun," Martha said as she gently hugged her daughter.

"Yes, and we could include some information about our church on the card," Pastor Randall added. "And, we can include the Gospel message to go along with the legend."

"That is a wonderful idea!" Jackie responded.

"Maybe some of the children can help to hand out the cards and candy canes," Pastor Randall suggested.

"Candy J's, Daddy," Cheryl reminded him.

"Yes, sorry, my Dear," Pastor Randall said as he teasingly poked at Cheryl's tummy and made her squirm and giggle.

"Now," Martha stated as she stood her daughter in front of her, "you go run along and play."

"Okay, Mommy," Cheryl replied as she skipped out of the room.

"We could even hang some candy canes on our Christmas tree in the main display at the town square," Chuck said.

"Yes, good idea." Jackie agreed. "And, that reminds me, we need to go to the tree farm on the outside of town and check on getting a tree."

"You want a real tree?" Chuck asked.

"Yes, I think that would be most effective for the main centerpiece display and for the photo backdrop. I want a large one, with large ornaments and large candy canes."

"It's a little too early to be buying a real tree now," Pastor Randall pointed out.

"Yes, I know," Jackie replied. "I just thought we could at least go ahead and get an idea of what we are looking for and the price. Maybe the tree farm will give us a good deal or even a donation since it is for the town."

"Good point," Chuck acknowledged.

"Maybe they will even let us go ahead and pick one out and reserve it," Jackie added.

"Good idea," Susan said.

"I can pick you up in my truck one evening after work, and we can look for it together," Chuck offered.

"Thank you, Chuck," Jackie said. "That would be great."

"I think it is so wonderful how the two of you are getting along so well and spending so much time together," Martha said with a big grin on her face.

Pastor Randall nudged her with his elbow and gave her a look as if to say, "Don't start on them again."

Jackie looked at Chuck and smiled. He smiled back.

"Perhaps we should get back to our festival planning," Pastor Randall said as an escape from the embarrassment of their friends.

They all laughed and then got back to work.

The remainder of that evening and the next few days were spent in building a list of potential vendors and advertising venues. They divided up the list and began contacting a few of them by email and their social media sites.

They met with widespread acceptance from potential vendors. Most seemed to think it was a great idea. A few of them said it was too far to travel to some small town they had never heard of. But, some said they had been looking for an avenue to open new doors for business expansion, and they were grateful for the opportunity.

Jackie posted about the festival on her social media little red truck group pages. The response was immediately overwhelming. Her red truck friends loved the idea. Some of them, who were vendors themselves, had been long awaiting an opportunity like this. Others, who were merely collectors, were surprised nothing like this had ever been done before. They hoped to be able to attend. Many of them even shared about the festival on their own pages to help spread the word.

The whole festival team was very encouraged with their initial success.

Chapter 5 - Tree Farm

Later that week, while on his lunch break at work, Chuck pulled his smart phone from his pocket. He opened the contacts app and selected Jackie's name.

After tapping on the send text message button, he typed, "O Christmas Tree, O Christmas Tree…", then he put his phone down on his desk.

A few seconds later, his phone vibrated, and he looked at the screen.

"U R 2 funny," the reply text said.

He picked his phone up and began typing once again. "Want to go tree hunting this evening?" Chuck typed.

"Sure!" came Jackie's reply.

"I have a stop to make after work, then I'll come get you," he typed.

"Ok. Sounds great!"

Chuck had barely put his phone back on his desk when it vibrated again.

He looked at the screen and saw, "XOXO".

Chuck smiled and tapped out "XOXO". He smiled again and pressed send.

He couldn't wait to see Jackie later that day.

The afternoon seemed to drag by. When quitting time finally arrived, Chuck darted for the door. He got in his truck and drove down the street a few blocks to the Division of Motor Vehicles. The parking lot was surprisingly empty, so Chuck parked in a space near the door. That was good. He hoped to get in and out quickly so that he could get over to Jackie's and then to the tree farm before they closed for the day.

Chuck hoped his friend, Shad, was working today and could help him with some information he wanted. He had not told Jackie about this trip to the DMV because he did not want to get her hopes up before he found out what he could learn.

He opened the door of the building and went in. No sooner had he set foot in the large customer area, when he heard a voice shout, "Hey, Chuck!"

He looked in the direction of the voice. It was his friend Shad, sitting behind a desk on the other end of the room. Chuck made his way in that direction.

"How are you doing, my friend?" Shad said as he stood up and held out his hand toward Chuck.

Chuck shook his hand and said, "I am

doing great. How have you been?”

“Great as well,” Shad answered. “What can I do for you?”

They both took a seat.

“I was hoping you could help me get some information,” Chuck began.

“Sure, what do you need?”

“I would like to find out more about the sale of a truck with this registration number.” Chuck removed a small piece of paper from his shirt pocket and handed it to his friend.

Shad typed a few things into the computer on his desk and clicked his mouse a few times.

“Wow, that must have been some time ago,” Shad stated.

“Yes, back in the early 50’s,” Chuck replied. “Do your records go back that far?”

“Yes,” Shad answered. “Let’s see if I can find the particular transaction you are looking for.”

After a few more clicks on his mouse,

he exclaimed, "Yes! Here it is! That truck changed owners only twice."

"That's what we thought," Chuck said.

"This shows the original owner and to whom he sold it, and for how much," Shad continued.

"That's awesome!" Chuck exclaimed.

"Let me write it all down for you," Shad said as he took a pen and small piece of paper out of his desk drawer.

He wrote the information on the paper and handed it to Chuck.

"Thank you so much," Chuck said as he looked at the information on the paper and then slid the paper down into his shirt pocket.

"We aim to please!" Shad said with a big grin.

"That was the fastest I ever got done at the DMV."

They both laughed.

Chuck was glad his friend saw the humor in his lame joke.

"Anything else I can do for you?" Shad asked

"No. I think that will do for this trip. That was a huge help. Thank you again."

"Anytime."

Chuck returned to his truck and headed for Jackie's home. He couldn't wait to let her know what he had found out.

Jackie was already on her front porch by the time Chuck drove down her long driveway. His truck had barely come to a stop when Jackie reached his passenger side door. Chuck loved her enthusiasm. She was like a kid in a candy store all the time.

Chuck hopped out of the truck to open the door for her. She paused, as if suddenly realizing what she was doing as she was about to open the door for herself.

"I can't get used to having someone open doors for me," Jackie said as she climbed into the truck. "You are spoiling me."

Chuck grinned as he closed her door. He came around to the other side and got in. Then, they headed down her driveway and onto the main road.

"How was work today?" Jackie asked.

"It was okay," Chuck answered. "I couldn't wait to get out of there."

"Where did you have to go after work?" she asked. "Before you picked me up."

"I was just about to tell you that," Chuck replied. "I have some information that I think you will find quite interesting."

"Tell me," Jackie said as she leaned closer across the seat. "I'm all ears."

"I stopped by the DMV," Chuck began. "I have a friend who works there."

He paused for a moment as he approached an intersection and checked for oncoming traffic before turning onto the next road.

"I had him check on the sale of your truck to your grandfather," he continued to explain.

"They can check back that far?" Jackie asked.

"Yes, and he found the record of the sales transaction."

"Awesome!" Jackie said excitedly. "So, did it say who sold him the truck?"

"A Samuel Miller sold it to your grandfather," Chuck answered.

"Here is the amount he sold it for," Chuck continued as he pulled the small piece of paper from his shirt pocket and handed it to Jackie.

"Cool! And, there is my grandfather's name too," Jackie said as she looked at the information that had been written on the paper.

"Wow, you could find out all of that?" Jackie asked with surprise in her voice.

"It pays to have friends in high places,"

Chuck stated. "Well, an old friend at the DMV, anyway."

Chuck smiled, and Jackie laughed at his humor.

"Thank you so much for getting this information," Jackie said. "It was so sweet of you to do that for me."

Jackie leaned across the seat toward Chuck and kissed his cheek.

Chuck smiled. "You're quite welcome. It's just one more clue in your mystery."

"That's true," she replied. "And, each step makes me want to find out even more."

"Here we are," Chuck said. "The tree farm."

He turned his truck into the dirt driveway of the farm. A sign near the edge of the road said, "Christmas Tree Farm - Fresh Cut Trees - Pine - Fir - Spruce".

"Looks like we are at the right place," Jackie said after she read the sign out loud.

Chuck pulled the truck up to the front

of a large red barn. It was the only structure near the parking area. There was a large farm house and other smaller buildings farther back on the property.

"I wonder if anyone is here," Chuck stated as they got out of the truck.

"Let's see if anyone is in the barn," Jackie suggested.

They walked through a large, open door in the barn and saw that there were lights on.

"Hello!" Chuck called out. "Anyone here?"

"I'll be right out!" a man's voice responded from the back.

After a brief moment, an older gentleman walked in from a door near the rear of the building. He was dressed in faded, denim overalls, work boots and a baseball cap.

"What can I do for you young folks?" the farmer asked.

"We want to select a Christms tree,"

Jackie replied.

"It's a little early to be getting a Christmas tree isn't it?" the farmer asked. "I've been running this Christmas tree farm for nearly 50 years now, and this is the earliest anyone has come looking for a tree." He followed his comment with a gruff but hearty laugh.

"We really just want to look around to see what is available," Chuck answered.

"And, maybe we can reserve one?" Jackie added as more of a request than a statement.

"You two must have kids who really love Christmas a lot!" the old farmer said and then laughed again.

Both Chuck and Jackie laughed as they looked toward each other.

"Did I say something wrong?" the farmer asked apologetically.

"We don't have children," Jackie answered. "We aren't married."

"Oh, my mistake," the farmer said. "I apologize."

"No problem," Chuck reassured him.

"We are actually wanting a tree for the town square," Jackie began to explain. "We are planning a Christmas festival to help boost the town's finances."

"Oh! Okay!" the farmer responded. "I understand. That sounds like a very worthy cause."

"We were wondering ..." Jackie's words were interrupted by the farmer.

"Don't worry," he said, "I will give you a good deal since it is for the town."

"Thank you, Sir!" Chuck replied.

"Yes, thank you!" Jackie added.

"Not a problem at all," the farmer said as he walked around to the back of what appeared to be a sales counter. He reached under the counter and brought out a bright red ribbon.

"You young folks help yourselves. Just

walk around the farm. When you find a tree you like, tie this ribbon onto one of its branches and write your name on this little tag attached to the end of the ribbon."

He handed the ribbon to Chuck and continued speaking before Chuck could thank him. "Make sure it's snug, so it doesn't blow off. The wind gets pretty fierce around here this time of year. And, take your time, there are a lot of trees out there."

"Thank you again," Chuck said.

"I'll make sure to hold onto the tree you select," the farmer added. "I'll take good care of it." He winked and smiled.

"Any tree you find is available," the farmer called out as they headed toward the door, "except the ones up near the house in the front yard. My wife likes those where they are." He laughed at his own attempt at humor.

Chuck and Jackie walked around the farm and were amazed at all of the trees.

There were so many, and each one seemed so well trimmed and shaped.

"He must spend a lot of time out here," Chuck pointed out. "Each tree looks like it is ready for someone's home."

"I was thinking the same thing," Jackie said.

As they inspected the trees, Jackie found several that she liked.

"We need to pick only one," Chuck said as he winked.

"I know," Jackie replied with a sigh. "It is such a hard decision. I find one I like, and then I find another one I think I like better than the previous one."

"I know what you mean. It reminds me of when I was a kid, and we would go tree hunting on a farm like this with my dad."

Chuck paused for a moment as he replayed some of those times in his mind. Then, he continued.

"My dad would tie a ribbon on a tree he

liked, and would keep looking for a better one. Then, he would send me back for the ribbon, so he could put it on the better selection."

"It sounds like he was worse than me," Jackie said with a laugh.

"You have no idea." Chuck also laughed as he rolled his eyes and shook his head. "It drove me crazy. They all looked practically the same to me. I just wanted to get back home."

Chuck paused again as they looked at a few more trees.

"I'm sure your dad just liked having you out there with him," Jackie said.

"Yes," Chuck replied. "Probably so. And, I should have appreciated it more myself. But, you know how kids are."

Chuck thought for a moment, and laughed.

"What is it?" Jackie asked.

"I just remembered something," Chuck

stated. "One year, he found a tree he liked and noticed that it had a praying mantis nest on one of its branches. He said he would leave it on there as it made an interesting decoration. I told him he better not leave it because it might hatch in the house. But, I was just a kid. What did I know?"

"Oh no," Jackie said. "I can see where this is going. He didn't, did he?"

"Yes, he left it on there. And, a few days after Christmas, we came home from somewhere, and the nest had hatched. There were hundreds - probably even thousands - of tiny, baby praying mantises all over the living room where we had the tree."

"Oh no! Yuck!"

"It was a mess," Chuck added.

"I'll bet it was!" Jackie said and then suddenly stopped walking. "O, Chuck, this is it! This is the one!"

"Yes, I do believe you are right," Chuck agreed as he looked at the tree directly in front of them. "That is a beauty, and it is just about the right height."

"It is lovely!" Jackie exclaimed. "Let's tie the ribbon on it."

Chuck tied the ribbon on one of the branches and made it as secure as he could.

"Is this a pine?" Jackie asked.

"Yes, a white pine."

"I almost forgot, we need to write our name on the tag," Jackie reminded him.

"Oh yes," Chuck replied.

"We don't have a pen," Jackie said.

"I have one here in my pocket," Chuck said as he removed the pen from his shirt pocket. He wrote their names on the tag and returned the pen to his pocket.

"Do you think we need to pay for it now?" Jackie asked.

"I'm not sure. Let's head back to the barn and let him know we found one, and we'll ask."

As they made their way back toward

the barn, Jackie placed her hand in Chuck's hand, and they walked hand-in-hand through the field. Chuck grinned as he realized that this was the first time they had actually held hands.

When they reached the barn, the farmer was outside, raking dry pine needles into a pile.

"Did you kids find a tree already?" he asked as he looked up and saw them coming.

"Yes, Sir," Chuck replied. "We marked it with the ribbon."

"Good and tight, I hope," the farmer said.

"Yes, Sir," Chuck acknowledged.

"Do we pay for it now, or later when we return to pick it up?" Jackie asked.

"You can pay for it later," the farmer answered. "It will be right there waiting for you. I hope you can find it again." He laughed.

"I hope so too," Chuck said with a

laugh.

"Could I ask you a question?" Jackie asked.

"I believe you just did," the farmer said. At that, he let out a loud belly laugh.

Jackie and Chuck laughed, and Chuck shook his head. "This guy reminds me of my dad," he thought to himself.

"I meant *another* question," Jackie explained with a smile before continuing with her question. "Do you know who owned the land across the road from your farm before the manufacturing plant bought it?"

"Yes, ma'am, little lady, I do." The farmer talked slowly, as if processing old memories as he spoke. "That land was a farm back then, in the 50's. It was owned by one of the previous mayors of our fair town."

He paused for a moment and seemed to be in thought.

"Do you know the mayor's name?" Jackie asked.

"I was just trying to recall that. I can't seem to get this old brain to remember back that far."

"Was his name Miller?" Chuck asked.

"Yes. I do believe that sounds about right," he answered before continuing his previous thought. "I never did know why the mayor sold his land to that manufacturing company and gave up his farm. But, it seemed like it was more of a hobby to him anyway. He didn't really need that farm for income. At least, that was my take on it."

"Thank you so much for the information," Jackie said as she held out her hand toward the farmer.

"You're quite welcome, young lady," he replied as he took off his work glove and shook her hand.

Chuck offered his hand, and the farmer shook it as he said, "You got yourself a pretty little lady here, young fella'. Take good care of her."

"I agree, Sir," Chuck said as he looked toward Jackie. "And, I will."

As they were pulling away in the truck, Chuck said, "So, that's why you wanted to come to the tree farm now, to talk to the owner about that land across the street."

He looked over at her and grinned to let her know he was only joking.

"Well sort of," Jackie replied. "I had hoped we might be able to get some more information for our mystery. But, I really did want to come pick out a tree."

Chuck laughed at her attempted defense.

"And, by the way," Jackie continued, "thank you for agreeing with the farmer's compliment back there. That was sweet of you."

"Oh, that," Chuck said with a smile after he realized what she meant. "You're welcome."

He reached over and took her hand and held it on the seat between them as the truck rolled down the road.

Chapter 6 - The Donation

The next evening, Chuck invited Jackie over to his place to do some online research together. They hoped to learn more about the town's history, thinking it could help not only with their mystery solving but with the festival planning as well.

"By the way," Jackie said as they were scrolling through search results on Chuck's computer, "my festival posts on my social media pages have gotten a lot of interest."

"That's great!" Chuck exclaimed.

"Many of my red truck friends think it is a great idea," Jackie continued, "and that it is a long time overdue to have something like this."

"I still can't believe it hasn't been done before," Chuck said.

"Me either," Jackie replied. "That is what my red truck friends think too. Some of them are actually planning to come, and a few from very far away, mainly because it is the first one. So, that is really working to our advantage."

"That's awesome," Chuck said as he clicked on a link on his screen.

"Those who are vendors and crafters are very excited to attend. Some have agreed to set up as vendors, and some want to just come check it out and make plans for future events and shows."

"And, there is another surprise I haven't told you yet," Jackie said.

"Oh, yeah?" Chuck asked as he

removed his hand from his computer's mouse and looked at Jackie to give her his full attention.

"I haven't told this to anyone yet," Jackie continued. "You will be the first to know."

"I'm honored," Chuck said with a smile and a slight head nod.

Jackie began to explain. "I emailed my favorite author and invited him to attend our festival. He has written several books centered around red truck themes. I didn't even expect to hear back from him. I'm sure he is busy and probably doing events all over the country. But, he replied!"

"Cool!" Chuck said. "What did he say?"

"He has agreed to come and do a book signing for all three days of our festival!"

Chuck could once again see the childlike excitement on Jackie's face and hear it in her voice.

"Wow, that is super cool!" he exclaimed. "You should share that with your red truck friends too."

"I will," Jackie replied. "That should certainly draw even more attention and interest. And, get this, he is going to post about his upcoming attendance at our festival on his own blog and social media sites!"

"Wow, that should help reach a lot of people," Chuck said.

"Yes," Jackie said. "I am so excited!"

"Really?" Chuck said jokingly. "I couldn't tell."

They both laughed, and Chuck continued scrolling in his web browser.

"Hey, I think I found something," he said after a few minutes. He turned his computer monitor to face a little more toward Jackie.

"There was a mayor of this town in the early 50's by the name of Samuel Miller."

"Wow!" Jackie said. "It just sunk in."

"What's that?" Chuck asked.

"My truck was probably owned by a mayor of our town," Jackie explained. "How cool is that?"

"That *is* pretty cool," Chuck said. "And here is some more information."

Chuck clicked to another page before continuing. "Another source shows that a man by that name also owned the land in question at one point around that same time period."

"Well, that confirms what the Christmas tree farmer told us," Jackie said. "I wonder when Mr. Miller sold it."

"I don't see that on here anywhere, but I'll bet the Planning Commission would have those records," Chuck suggested.

"Do you have a friend who works there too?" Jackie asked playfully.

"No, but I'll bet Susan could help us with that."

"True," Jackie replied. "I'm sure she

can do that."

Chuck was about to click off of that page when Jackie said, "Wait!"

"What is it?" Chuck asked.

"Look at this," Jackie answered as she pointed to a line of text farther down the page on the computer screen.

"This says the town was in trouble financially during Miller's term of office," Jackie explained. "And, a big donation came in that saved the town from bankruptcy."

"I wonder who gave the donation," Chuck said.

"It looks like it was an anonymous donation," Jackie said as she scrolled down the page using Chuck's mouse.

"The mystery just keeps growing," Chuck said.

Chapter 7 - Opposition

The Town Council met weekly on Monday nights in the Town Hall building, and Susan always tried to be there early. As mayor of their town, she presided over the meetings. She was excited on this particular night, as she would be sharing the idea about the festival.

Susan entered the large meeting room and switched on the lights. It seemed like such a cold, lonely place when it was empty, but it could get quite lively when controversial topics were discussed.

She approached the large, seven-seat desk at the front of the room. It always reminded her of a large judge's bench in a courtroom but with seven seats rather than just one. She took her customary seat in the center chair.

As the other six members began to arrive, they exchanged their usual greetings and took their seats.

Other people from town began to arrive as well. There was usually only a small number of citizens in attendance, consisting mostly of local newspaper, radio and television reporters. But, when controversial topics were on the agenda, the room was sometimes filled to standing room only. Those meetings could get quite lengthy, as members of the community would present arguments and presentations for or against certain issues that concerned them.

Susan did not expect a large crowd for

this evening's meeting, and she hoped it would be a short one. The only item of new business on the agenda that she was aware of was the festival, and she expected that discussion to go very smoothly and quickly.

When the council members were all present and assembled and the official time for the meeting arrived, Susan called the meeting to order.

They proceeded through the regular meeting agenda, which included the reading and approval of the minutes from the previous meeting. The treasurer's report was then distributed and discussed. That was once again a rather dismal discussion due to the town's bleak financial situation. And then, old business items which were still outstanding were discussed.

The time for new business finally arrived, and Susan asked if anyone had any items to bring before the council. She wanted to give others an opportunity to share their items before she shared about the festival.

"I have an item," one of the members said in a rather gruff voice. "It is more like a concern."

His name was Gerald Krofton. He was an older member of the council who had served many terms. As a wealthy businessman in the town, he had much influence and power in their small community. He usually opposed anything Susan presented or suggested. And, he seemed to hold a great amount of influence over several of the other members as well.

"Please share your concern, Mr. Krofton," Susan said rather hesitantly.

"I have heard reports of a festival being planned for our town," Krofton continued. "We have not approved any such festival. Am I correct?"

Several other council members verbally confirmed his statement. They had not approved such an event. It had never even been discussed.

Susan had not expected that. Although, it really did not surprise her, coming from Mr. Krofton. But, she did wonder how he had found out about it already.

"Let me explain," Susan began, "as that was the next item on the agenda anyway."

She collected her thoughts and said a quick, silent prayer before beginning. "Several members of our community came up with an idea to help our town's financial difficulty."

"A problem that you, as mayor, helped to cause," Mr. Krofton grumbled.

Susan ignored the interruption and continued, "We thought a Christmas festival might help to stimulate the economy as well as build public recognition for our town. We chose the very popular little red truck as a theme. We are calling it the 'Little Red Truck Christmas Festival'. We plan to have craft vendors and ..."

Her explanation was once again sharply interrupted by Mr. Krofton. "How is a craft show going to help save the town's finances?"

Several of the other members laughed in agreement.

"And, who is even interested in little red trucks anymore," another member stated. "That fad is dead."

"Just a bunch of housewives who like red trucks on pillows," another member added.

Several of the members laughed once again.

Susan once again tried to ignore the rude comments and press on with her presentation. "It is way more than that," she continued. "Red trucks are actually growing in popularity all across the country. And, they are valued by more than just 'housewives'." Susan used her fingers to make air quotes.

"Books are even being written about them," she continued. "Plus, the event we are planning is more than just being about red trucks. It is a Christmas festival, primarily. Red trucks are just the theme to set the stage and attract vendors and collectors."

"Notice she said they are *planning* the festival," Mr. Krofton once again interrupted. "They are planning a festival that has not even been approved by the Town Council."

"No one can have a town-wide festival without the council's approval," another member pointed out. "You are fully aware of that. Are you not, Miss Wellers?"

"Yes, I am aware of that," Susan replied after saying another silent prayer asking for wisdom and patience. "That is precisely why I am bringing it before you now. We only started the planning since the time is so very short."

"I think it is a great idea," one of the other members stated. "It would certainly bring in revenue and awareness for our town."

"We need to vote on it," Mr. Krofton angrily demanded.

"We need time to digest all of this," another member said. "I suggest we convene again tomorrow night to decide by vote. That will give us time to think about it."

"What a waste of time," Krofton grumbled. "We should vote now and get this over with."

"I agree that we need time to consider the proposal," another member added.

"Is everyone in agreement that we will meet again tomorrow night to put this to a vote?" Susan asked in an attempt to get this ended, at least for now.

They all agreed although some rather reluctantly.

"Okay," Susan continued. "We will meet here tomorrow night at the same time. Does anyone have anything else for tonight's meeting before we adjourn?"

Susan sure hoped no one had any other items for discussion. She just wanted to get out of there and go cry.

No one spoke up, so Susan said, "Then this meeting is adjourned. See you all tomorrow night."

Susan hurried to her car and just sat there for a few minutes. As she replayed the meeting in her mind, tears welled up in her eyes.

"I really messed up this time," she thought to herself. "I shouldn't have agreed to have the festival without getting approval from the council first. I just got so caught up in the excitement about the idea. I allowed my friends to believe it would happen, and now I'll be letting them down if the vote goes negative."

She tried to stop the discouraging thoughts from filling her mind, but they kept coming. She cupped her hands over her face and cried.

After a few minutes, she pulled herself together, wiped her eyes with a tissue and removed her phone from her purse. She dialed Jackie's number but paused before pressing the send button.

She really did not have the heart to tell Jackie the bad news, but felt she should, especially since she had noticed a few reporters in the room at the meeting. It would probably be in tomorrow's paper. And, she knew how Mr. Krofton and his camp had the media tied around their little fingers.

She pressed the send button and listened to it ring a couple times.

"Hey, Susan!" Jackie answered on the other end. "Wasn't your council meeting tonight? How did it go?"

"Can I meet with you and Chuck right away?" Her voice cracked a little, and she was afraid it would give away her disappointment.

"Susan, what's wrong?" Jackie asked

with obvious concern in her voice.

"Everything's okay," Susan said, trying to sound reassuring. It wasn't exactly a lie. It was at least her hope that everything was, in fact, okay. "I will explain when we get together."

"Okay," Jackie replied. "Do you want to meet here at my house?"

"Yes, that will be fine if it suits you."

"Absolutely! I'll call Chuck and have him meet us here," Jackie offered.

"Okay, thank you. I will see you in a few minutes."

When she arrived at Jackie's house, she prayed before getting out of her car. "Please, Lord, help me to hold it together in there. And, please, help them to not be too disappointed."

Jackie met her at the door, and they both went in together. Chuck was already there.

They sat in the living room, and Susan

began to explain about the meeting. She told them how the discussion had gone and how negative some of the council members had been toward the idea of the festival.

"Some of them would love to stop it from happening," Susan stated, "just to flex their political power."

"They can't do that," Jackie said emphatically. "We have worked so hard."

"I am so sorry," Susan said. "I thought they would embrace the idea. I should have known Mr. Krofton would be a stumbling block, as always."

"It's not your fault," Jackie said.

"I just never dreamed it would be a problem," Susan continued. "I thought they would go for an idea to save the town, especially when we were doing most, if not all, of the work. It was such a great idea that I focused more on the excitement and possible results than I did on the approval process and my responsibility as mayor and chairwoman of the town council.”

“Sounds like a political power move to me,” Chuck said.

“You are right about that,” Susan replied. “It’s only because some of them are against my conservative political views. They have resented me ever since I got elected, mainly because I’m a Christian. I just never thought they would actually vote against a plan to help the town simply to fight me politically.”

“They probably want to ruin your chances of getting re-elected,” Jackie said. “If the town fails on your watch, so to speak, they will get their way and get their own candidate elected.”

“Exactly,” Susan responded.

“That is just wrong,” Chuck said.

“Maybe having the festival wasn’t such a good idea after all,” Jackie said with discouragement in her voice and in her eyes.

“It is still a great idea,” Susan said.

“They cannot change that fact.”

“We are talking like they already voted to cancel the plans,” Chuck pointed out. “It isn’t over yet. We will all be praying for the vote tomorrow night.”

“I’ll call Pastor Randall and Martha and let them know what’s going on and ask them to pray too,” Jackie offered.

“Thank you, both,” Susan said as she dabbed her eyes with a tissue.

Chapter 8 - Indecision

Susan arrived at the Town Council meeting room even earlier than normal the following night. She wanted to spend some time praying over the meeting and the vote.

"Lord, You know my will in this, and the will of my friends, and the financial need our town has," she prayed out loud. "But, we really do want Your will to be done, not ours. Direct the vote to accomplish Your will. I know that You are in control, and that You have a purpose in all of this. You have plans we may not even be aware of. Guide and direct us in order to fulfill those plans. And, please help our discussions to be peaceful tonight. Thank You, Lord. In Jesus' Name. Amen."

Just as she finished her prayer, she heard the rear door open. The other council members began to enter the room. Susan waited for everyone to take their seats.

"Well, let's get this over with!" Mr. Krofton practically shouted. "No use wasting any more time than necessary."

"I call this special meeting to order," Susan stated. "The purpose of this meeting is to vote on the proposal of having a Christmas festival to support our town's finances."

"We all know why we are here," Krofton remarked. "Get on with the vote."

"All in favor of having the festival, please raise your right hand," Susan said.

Susan raised her hand, and two of the other members did the same. Susan's heart sank. It was going to be three in favor and four against. They had lost.

"All against having the festival, please raise your right hand," she said with obvious discouragement in her voice.

To her surprise, only three of the remaining council members raised their hands, one of which was Mr. Krofton, of course. One member, Dave Ashton, had not voted for either choice.

"Dave, you didn't vote," Susan said, stating what was probably already apparent to everyone in the room.

"I am really too undecided," Dave explained. "I see the point of both sides. I just don't know which one is right."

Dave was a younger, less experienced council member. He was a business owner in town, and this was his first term serving on the council, or in any government position for that matter. Dave often asked many questions to help him in making decisions before voting. He never wanted to jump into things without the proper information. Susan respected him for that.

"For crying out loud, Ashton!" Mr. Krofton yelled from his end of the bench. "You know the festival would be nothing but a waste of time and a huge expense and embarrassment to our town. Just vote against it and let's get out of here."

"I'm sorry," Dave said sincerely, "but, I need more time to think. One day was not enough time."

"I can appreciate that, Dave," Susan said. "If anyone needs more information, please ask. I will share all I know. For now, perhaps we should postpone our vote since we have a tie at this point. We can vote again at our regular meeting next Monday. That will give everyone a week - well, almost a week - to decide."

"Oh, for Pete's sake!" Krofton grumbled as he folded his arms across his chest.

Wanting to speed the process, Susan said, "All in favor of postponing our vote until next Monday's meeting, raise your right hand."

Five members raised their hands, including one who had voted against the festival to begin with. But, that hand quickly went down with a scowl from Mr. Krofton toward that council member.

"That is four votes in favor of postponing," Susan said. "At least we have a majority agreeing to postpone. So, postpone we shall. This meeting is adjourned. See you all next Monday night."

When Susan reached her car, she took out her cell phone. She selected Jackie's entry in her contact list and paused before pressing the dial button.

"I really don't want to give them this bad news again," she thought to herself. "But, it could have been worse."

She pressed the dial button, and after a couple rings, Jackie answered.

"Hey, Susan! That was a short meeting! That must mean good news!"

"Well, not exactly," Susan replied. "Is Chuck there with you?"

"Yes. Let me put my phone on speaker so he can hear."

"Hi Susan," Chuck said.

"Hey Chuck."

"So, how did the vote go?" Jackie asked.

"We actually had a tie vote," Susan began to explain.

"How can you have a tie?" Chuck asked. "I thought there were seven members on the council."

"One of them was undecided," Susan answered. "He needs more time to think. We had to postpone the vote for another week, until next Monday's meeting."

"Oh, no!" Jackie said.

"Well, at least it was not totally killed yet," Chuck said.

"True," Susan replied. "But, I am afraid that the undecided member is facing pressure from the opposing side. I know him. I feel certain that he wants to vote in favor of the festival but is afraid to do so. And, even worse, he knows his is the tie breaking vote."

"And, now there is time for the opposing side to pressure him even more," Jackie said.

"We just have to pray that doesn't happen," Chuck said, "and that some of the other members will get a clue before next Monday."

"I am so sorry for leading you all into all of this without first going through the proper channels," Susan said.

"God can still make a way," Chuck said. "We need to pray. Let's all meet at the church."

"Good idea," Jackie said. "I'll call

Pastor Randall and Martha."

"We will meet you there in 15 minutes," Jackie said.

"Okay, see you then," Susan replied. "And, thank you both."

Chuck and Jackie arrived at the church just as Pastor Randall and Martha were going through the front door. Susan pulled into the parking lot right behind them.

After they all went into the church building, they explained everything to the pastor and his wife and then spent some time in prayer. Then, they discussed the situation a little more and decided to continue with their plans as if everything was on.

"We have another rehearsal for the Christmas drama scheduled for this coming Sunday night," Martha said. "We need to be prepared if we do have it."

"Yes," Susan said. "If we have the festival, we need to be ready. If we don't have it …." She paused for a moment, as if not able to get the words out.

"If we don't have it," Jackie continued for her, "then we don't have it. We will move forward in faith that the Lord will make a way."

"Agreed," Susan said.

"Agreed," everyone else said in unison.

After Pastor Randall and Martha had left, Chuck and Jackie remained standing in the parking lot with Susan.

"Do you have a minute, Susan?" Jackie asked.

"Sure," Susan replied. "What's up?"

"We have a mystery to solve," Chuck said, "and we need your help."

Jackie explained to her about their findings concerning the land sale and the donation that saved the town all those years ago.

"The town could use another donation

like that, right about now," Susan said, trying to lighten the mood. "How can I help in your mystery?"

"We were wondering if you could help us search the records at the Planning Commission," Chuck said.

"We apologize for bothering you with this," Jackie added. "We know you have other things on your mind right now."

"Nonsense," Susan said. "I would be glad to help. Besides, it will serve as a nice distraction from everything else. Can you two meet me at the Town Hall building tomorrow?"

"I can go after work," Chuck said, "if that suits the two of you."

"Suits me," Jackie stated.

"Fine with me," Susan also agreed.

"I'll try to get off a little early so we have time before it closes," Chuck offered.

"I have a key," Susan said with a grin. "So, you don't have to hurry. We can just meet after you get off work.”

“Sounds great,” Chuck said.

“Thank you, Susan,” Jackie added.

“You’re welcome, my friends,” Susan replied. “I just hope I can be of some help. Solving a mystery sounds like fun!”

They all laughed as they headed toward their vehicles.

Chapter 9 - Falling Into Place

The following day, after work, Chuck picked up Jackie, and they headed toward the center of town where the Town Hall building was located. They hoped they did not keep Susan waiting too long.

"It is really nice of her to help us like this," Jackie said. "With her being the mayor, I am sure she is quite busy."

"Yes, I can't imagine the pressures she faces every day," Chuck added. "I'm sure our little mystery seems pretty insignificant compared to other things she has to deal with."

"And, speaking of our mystery," Jackie continued, "thank you for all of your help too."

"You are very welcome," Chuck replied. "It has been my pleasure to help. But, we haven't solved it all yet."

"True," Jackie agreed. "But, whether or not we solve it, I appreciate the help you have given me. I know it's not important that we find any answers to all of this, but I just want to know."

"I understand," Chuck acknowledged. "I feel the same way. The more we learn, the more I want to find out."

"Exactly."

When they arrived at the Town Hall building, Susan was standing just inside the glass doors. She opened the door for them, and they went inside.

"The Planning Commission office is just down this way," Susan said as she headed down the long hallway. They followed her, which was at quite a fast pace.

"I hope we didn't keep you waiting long," Jackie said.

"No, not at all," Susan replied, barely lessening her stride. "I had just arrived shortly before you two did."

She stopped in front of a door that had the words "Planning Commision" on the glass window.

"Here we are," she said as she opened the door and motioned for them to enter.

They followed her across the large room which was filled with desks and filing cabinets. There was a man working at a desk near one of the side walls. He was the only other person in the room, as it was after normal business hours.

Susan headed in his direction and stopped in front of his desk.

"Hello, Madam Mayor," the man said as he stood to his feet.

"Hi, Eric," Susan said. "These are my friends that I told you about. Jackie and Chuck."

"Pleased to meet you both," he replied.

"And, this is Eric Branson," Susan continued with the introductions. "I asked him to stay today and see if he could give us some assistance in your search."

"Thank you," Jackie said. "That is mighty nice of you."

"No problem," Eric responded. "So, tell me more about this search of yours. Mayor Susan already told me a little, but not the finer details."

Jackie explained to him about her grandfather's truck and the registration paper she had found with the other name on it. She also told him about the address being near where the manufacturing plant is located now and about the signs of the abandoned entranceway.

"Why would the address not be the same as the manufacturing plant's address if it is, in fact, the same piece of land?" she asked. "And, why would it not show up on my map app?" Jackie asked.

"Because the guys in vehicle registration probably got the address wrong," Eric replied.

He paused for a moment and then laughed. "No, I'm only kidding," he explained. "Just a little rivalry between our departments."

"Oh, good," Jackie said. "I thought you were serious, and we would be at a dead end."

"No, there is a very reasonable explanation as to the apparent disparity in the addresses."

"He loves using big words," Susan said with a grin.

"When we changed the addressing

system for the 911 service," Eric began to explain, "we blocked them off in 5.28 feet increments.   That way, the emergency responders know exactly where a residence is located based on its address, and they know how far down the road it is."

"That makes sense," Chuck said. "I didn't realize it was so precise. But, 5.28 feet? Why such an odd number?"

"That's actually an *even* number," Eric answered before pausing. "Sorry, math joke."

"I should have seen that one coming," Chuck said with a laugh. "I'm an accountant."

"Too funny," Eric replied. "Well, to answer your question, 5.28 feet means there would be one thousand potential addresses per one mile of road."

"Oh, okay," Chuck said. "Again, that makes sense."

"Yes," Eric acknowledged, and then he continued with his explanation. "So, if the entrance of the manufacturing plant is farther down the road than the old driveway of the previous residence, then the actual physical address would have changed."

"Now I understand," Jackie stated. "Thank you for the explanation."

"You're welcome," Eric replied as he typed on his computer keyboard. "Now, let me see if I can find … yes, here it is."

"What did you find?" Susan asked.

"I searched in the land deeds and sales transactions and found that particular parcel of land. Here is where it was sold to the manufacturing company before they built their plant. It was sold for quite a substantial amount of mulah."

He pointed to the dollar amount on the screen and Jackie leaned in for a closer look.

"Wow, that *is* a lot!" Jackie said. "Hey, look at the date of the transaction." She pointed to the date that was displayed on the screen to the left of the amount.

"Interesting," Chuck said. "The date of the land transaction was only a few days before the sale of your truck. I guess he didn't need the truck if he sold his farm."

"And, the date the donation was given to the town was immediately after that," Jackie said.

"The clues to your mystery are beginning to fall into place," Chuck said.

"He must have sold the land and given the money to the town," Susan said.

"It sure looks that way," Chuck agreed. "Now, that's commitment."

"But wait," Jackie said, "the amount of the donation was more than the sale of the land."

Everyone was silent for a moment, and then Chuck spoke up. "Remember the amount he sold his truck to your grandfather for?"

"Yes," Jackie said, and then she paused in thought. "That amount completes the total of the donation!"

"So, the sale of his land and the sale of his truck to your grandfather saved the town," Susan said. "How grand! What a great mystery you have solved!"

"Thanks to all of you and your help,": Jackie said. Then she paused as if in thought. "We should honor Mr. Miller at the festival in some way."

"That would be great," Chuck said, "But, he apparently didn't want anyone to know. He gave the donation anonymously, and he has kept it a secret for all these years. Maybe we should keep it that way."

"True, good point," Jackie somewhat reluctantly agreed. "I just wish there was something we could do to honor him or thank him or something, especially after you all went to so much trouble to help me solve this whole thing."

"I have an idea," Susan spoke up cheerfully.

"What is it?" Jakie asked in eager

anticipation.

"I'll tell you about it later," Susan answered. "Let me work out some details first."

"Okay," Jackie replied. "We solved one mystery, we might as well have another."

They all laughed.

When everyone had left the Town Hall building, and Chuck and Jackie were back in his truck, Jackie said, "You were right."

"About what?" Chuck asked.

"All of the clues did fall into place," she answered. "Thank you for all your help."

"You're welcome," Chuck replied.

"Speaking of falling into place," Jackie continued, "since we finished getting my truck ready, can we go ahead and take it over to the town square and display it there? At least that much will be done in the event that the council approves the festival."

"Sure! We can do that."

Chapter 10 - Decisions

Sunday night, Dave Ashton walked through the center of downtown. He merely wanted to get some fresh air so he could think. He had been wrestling with his decision for the vote ever since the meeting on Tuesday night. His decision had to be made by the following night when the council met again.

The arguments from both sides tossed back and forth in his mind, and he could not get a clear answer either way. They both had merit in his mind.

Having a festival to help the town's financial situation seemed to make a lot of sense to Dave. However, he also knew the trouble that Gerald Krofton and his side could cause for him if he voted in favor of the festival and against them. Dave did not want to vote based on fear, but he had a business to run. He didn't have the pull that they did in town.

As he walked toward the town square, he noticed a small group of people gathered there. He walked closer and saw that it was mainly young people - middle school or high school aged kids. They seemed to be rehearsing for some sort of drama production.

Dave went closer to investigate, thinking it might at least give him a distraction from his current troubles.

The props and set that were strategically placed on the concrete slab of the town square looked like a Nativity scene. He remembered similar scenes from his church's Christmas programs years ago.

The stable was a simple, roughly built wooden frame. There was a wooden manger filled with straw positioned just in front of the structure. A plastic doll in the manger served as Baby Jesus.

Dave also noticed there was an old, unrestored truck near the stone wall at the other end of the concrete slab. For the Red Truck Festival, he assumed.

"They could have at least used a more restored truck," he thought to himself. "And, more red rather than rusty."

Some of the young people were dressed in costumes depicting Biblical characters. He could distinguish Mary and Joseph standing together off to one side with several angels. There were also a few shepherds with the tell-tale shepherds' hooks. One of them was holding a stuffed lamb in his arms.

But, there was something missing, he thought. "Oh yes, the three wisemen," he said to himself when he realized those particular characters were nowhere to be seen. "Aren't they supposed to be here too?"

Dave took a seat on a nearby park bench and listened as a woman began to speak to the youth.

Martha explained to her drama team that they would be performing the drama story several times on each of the three days of the festival. That would give them many opportunities to reach more people throughout the weekend.

She told them that her daughter, Cheryl, and some other children from the church family would be handing out Candy J's along with cards explaining the legend of the candy cane and the gospel message.

"Some of you have your costumes already," Martha continued. "Please be careful while wearing them. No food or drink while you have them on. We will have the rest of your costumes ready by our next practice, hopefully. Okay, everyone, get in your places. Let's start at the beginning and run through the whole thing."

They proceeded to act out the scenes from the second chapter of Luke's gospel while several of the youth took turns reading the familiar passage.

When they finished the verse that told of the shepherds returning and praising God and telling everyone about what they had seen and heard, Martha turned to her husband. "This is when you will give your message," she told him.

As Pastor Randall stepped forward, he noticed Dave sitting on the bench. He stepped back, leaned close to Martha and spoke quietly into her ear so no one else could hear.

"Do you know who that man over there

is?" he asked her.

"No, I don't," she answered. "I saw him walk over and sit down a few minutes ago."

"I don't know who he is either," Pastor Randall continued. "So, I am going to go ahead and give my complete message instead of just skipping it for practice. At least, most of it. Will that be okay?"

"Great idea," Martha replied. "Yes, that will be fine. I'll be praying for you, and for him."

"Thank you, Dear," he said as he stepped forward once again.

Pastor Randall began speaking, doing his best to project his voice to be heard by anyone who might be around. "Good evening, everyone. My name is Pastor Randall. The youth from our church have just presented to you the story of the Nativity, the birth of Jesus.

"The shepherds who were visited by

the angel on that holy night rejoiced because they recognized the gift from the Lord they had just witnessed and received in that lowly stable. As the angel told them, a Savior had been born to them that day.

"John 3:16 tells us more about that wonderful gift of salvation from God. That verse says,

'*For God so loved the world that he gave his one and only Son, that whoever believes in him shall not perish but have eternal life.*'

"That is the true reason for this season," Pastor Randall stated. "God loved us so much that He gave His own Son to die in our place for our sins. And, all we have to do is believe in Him to receive the gift of eternal life.

"You may have wondered why the wise men are not present at our Nativity scene," Pastor Randall continued. "They actually did not arrive until a couple years later. And, they went to the house the family was staying in at the time, not to the stable. But, do you remember the gifts they brought? Gold, frankincense and myrrh. Those were very valuable items. They were very precious gifts."

He paused for a moment before continuing. "God gave an even greater and more precious gift - His Son. It is said that wise men still seek Him today."

Pastor Randall smiled and then said, "I know that is an overused statement, but it still rings true. The decision to accept Jesus as Savior is the most important decision anyone will ever make. If you have never made that decision, I hope you will do so today. Accept the wonderful gift that God is offering to you."

"Or, perhaps you have already accepted Jesus as Savior," Pastor Randall added.

"Maybe you accepted Him years ago, but you have fallen away. Perhaps your dedication to following Him has waned. The decision you face now would be to commit to following Him in all you do from this night forward."

Pastor Randall was about to lead in a prayer of salvation when he was impressed to say one more thing first.

"Whatever your decision is, ask the Lord to help you. It is your choice, but He will help you and guide you."

The pastor's words repeated in Dave's mind. "Decision. Your choice."

It was like he was speaking directly to him, as if he knew what was on his mind at this very moment.

Pastor Randall led in a prayer. He asked the Lord to help his listeners to make the right decision - to either accept God's indescribable gift of salvation through Jesus or to recommit to following Him. And, like the shepherds, to go tell others the good news about Jesus.

Dave didn't hear many of the words Pastor Randall prayed. The word 'decision' kept echoing in his mind. He knew he had some decisions to make, and they were not all for the following night's meeting.

"Lord, I know it has been a while since I accepted Jesus as my Savior," Dave prayed in his heart. "I have not been living my life for you totally as I should. I had forgotten the true joy of Christmas. I have failed to live my life for You and for Your purposes. Please forgive me. Use me, I pray. Help me to make every decision for Your glory. Amen."

When he looked up, he saw the pastor walking toward him.

"I'm Pastor Randall," the pastor said as he extended his hand toward Dave.

Dave shook the pastor's hand and said,

"I'm Dave."

"Good to meet you, Dave."

"You too, Pastor".

"I noticed you have been sitting here for a while this evening," Pastor Randall said. "Is there anything I can do for you?"

Dave hesitated before speaking, and then he said, "Thank you for your message tonight."

"You're welcome. I wasn't planning to give the entire message tonight since this was only a practice," Pastor Randall explained. "But, the Lord prompted me to go ahead and share it all."

"I'm glad you did," Dave replied. "I needed to hear it. I realized tonight that I needed to make the decision to recommit my life to the Lord. I was saved many years ago when I was in college. But, I feel like I lost my salvation somewhere along the way. I'm ashamed to say it, but I fell away from attending church and stopped reading my

Bible. Not for any particular reason. I just got distracted by everything else.”

“Well, first let me say, thank you for sharing that with me.” Pastor Randall prayerfully selected his words before continuing. “Let me explain something that might help.”

“Okay, please do,” Dave replied.

“If you were truly saved all those years ago, and I do not doubt that you were, then nothing can take that away from you.”

“Really?” Dave asked.

“Yes, really. Do you see that old, vintage truck sitting over there?” Pastor Randall pointed to Jackie’s truck that was waiting for the rest of the main display to be added later.

“Yes, quite an old relic, it seems,” Dave said. “Why is it there?”

“It’s actually part of a display for the Christmas festival we are planning,” Pastor Randall answered. “The rest of the display will be set up later.”

“Oh, okay.”

“But, you are right, it is quite old,” Pastor Randall continued. “It has lost its shine. It has lost its original color and finish and has not functioned as an actual truck for quite some time. It actually serves as a decoration. But, is it any less of a truck than when it was made back in the 50’s on the manufacturing line?”

“No, I guess not,” Dave answered.

“Is it still a truck?” Pastor Randall asked.

“Yes, of course.”

“Exactly,” Pastor Randall stated. “Once we are saved, and God’s seal is on us, we might fall away from our calling and purpose. We might even lose our shine for the Lord. But, we still belong to Him. His seal is on us. We are still His children whether we act like it or not.”

“That makes sense,” Dave replied.

"Besides," Pastor Randall added, "if we could do anything to *lose* our salvation, that would mean we have to *earn* it as well."

"Oh, yes," Dave interjected before the pastor could finish his explanation. "I get it. Salvation is a free gift from God. We cannot earn it."

"Exactly! Ephesians 2, verses 8 and 9 tell us that we are saved by grace through faith and not by works. So, if works cannot save us, then a lack of works, or an abundance of bad actions, cannot lose it for us either."

"Good point," Dave stated.

"We are not perfect. God is constantly in the process of restoring us and making us new," Pastor Randall continued. "He saves us, and we become the righteousness of Christ. That is in 2 Corinthians 5:21. It is quite a mystery and beyond our human understanding that His Son became sin for us, so that we could become His righteousness."

"Yes, that is quite a mystery," Dave replied.

"God then begins to change us," Pastor Randall continued, "to transform us into His image through the work of His Holy Spirit within us. That is the sanctification process. Another mystery of God's working. So, you see, salvation and sanctification are two different things."

"Yes, I see that now," Dave replied. "Thank you, Pastor. I understand. That helps a lot."

"You are welcome to join us any time at our church. It is just outside of town."

"Yes, I know where it is," Dave said. "And, thank you again."

"You're welcome. God bless you, my friend."

"God bless you too."

As Pastor Randall rejoined his group up front, Dave remembered the problem that had brought him out here on this particular evening. He had another decision to make. And, he now knew what that choice needed to be, no matter what certain other council members thought.

Chapter 11 - The Vote

Monday night finally arrived, and Susan once again took her seat in the council meeting room. There was a larger crowd present this time. Word had undoubtedly gotten out. People loved controversy, at least when they weren't directly involved. It seemed to serve as a warped source of entertainment.

Susan called the meeting to order, and they proceeded through their regular Monday night agenda. When they reached the time for old business, she almost dreaded bringing it up again for fear of the result.

"The only old business I am aware of is our pending vote on the town Christmas festival," she announced.

"The *Little Red Truck* Festival," one of the council members said in a very sarcastic tone of voice.

"The Little Red Truck *Christmas* Festival," Susan corrected as kindly as she could bear. "Are we ready to vote?"

"I saw that old truck sitting in the town square," Gerald Krofton scoffed. "Is that your idea of decorating for the festival? An old, junker truck? It's an eye-sore. It's an embarrassment."

Another member voiced his agreement with Krofton.

"That is only part of a main display that will be present for visitors to take photos with," Susan explained. "Many people appreciate the vintage look."

"Let's just vote and get this done," Krofton grumbled.

"All in favor of moving ahead with the festival, please signify by raising your right hand," Susan instructed.

Susan was shocked, but delighted, when three hands in addition to hers went up. Dave Ashton was included in that count this time.

"This is bogus!" Krofton shouted, not allowing for the opposing vote.

One of the other members, who had previously voted against the festival, asked Dave why he had decided to vote in favor of the motion this time.

Dave shared some of what he had seen and heard the night before at the drama rehearsal in the town square. He told about the youth Christmas drama and about the pastor's message.

"I had lost my focus on what the true message of Christmas really is," Dave continued. "I had forgotten who I was called to be and realized this festival is what we all need. Maybe we can all see the true meaning of Christmas, along with helping the town at the same time. It's a win-win."

"That's all we need on the council, another religious fanatic!" Krofton shouted. He stood from his seat and stormed out of the room.

The spectators became roused at the disruption, and the noise level in the room rose significantly.

"Please, everyone, settle down!" Susan said to regain some order. "We still have a matter up for vote."

"I'm sorry to cause an uproar," Dave apologized. "But, religious fanatic or not, I believe having the festival is the right thing to do. It is exactly what this town needs. It's what we *all* need. This can be our gift to the town."

"I agree. I vote in favor of the

festival.”

“So do I.”

It was the remaining two members who had spoken up and raised their right hands. Now, it was six votes in favor of the motion.

Susan was so shocked she almost forgot to close the vote. But, she came to herself and pounded her gavel on its wooden base. “The motion carries. We will have the festival as planned! And, with that, if there is no new business, this meeting is adjourned!”

No one had any new business, so they began to dismiss.

“Thank you, Dave,” Susan said as she stood from her seat.

“You’re welcome,” he replied. “Thank you all for all you’ve done. And, if there is anything I can do to help with the festival, be sure to let me know.”

“We will, thank you.”

Susan practically ran to her car, and

when she got there, she pulled out her phone to call Jackie. She could not wait to tell her friend the good news.

Jackie had barely answered the phone when Susan shouted, "They approved it! We can have the festival!"

"That is great news!" Jackie replied. "Praise the Lord!"

"Praise Him, indeed!" Susan said. "That was nothing short of a miracle!"

"What swayed the undecided member to vote in favor of the festival?" Jackie asked. "Do you know?"

Susan told her what Dave had shared about the drama rehearsal in the town square, and how he had decided what the right decision was.

"And, it wasn't just him," Susan continued. "After Dave shared his reason for voting in favor of the festival, two of the other members, who had previously voted against the festival, voted in favor of having it this time."

"Wow!" Jackie responded. "An even bigger 'Praise the Lord!'"

"Amen!" Susan agreed. "Can you tell Chuck and the others?"

"I would be glad to!" Jackie replied. "Thank you for letting me know the good news."

"You're welcome."

Jackie called Chuck and then Martha right away. She was so excited. They could finally finish the remaining plans. With the festival weekend nearly upon them, time was of the essence.

They all agreed to meet the following evening to make final preparations and to make sure no details had been missed.

Chapter 12 - The Festival

Chuck drove slowly into town as he took in all of the sights. Since his truck was being used in the festival display, he was in his car.

The first two days of the Little Red Truck Christmas Festival had come and gone with huge success. Chuck had been so busy helping Jackie and the others that he had not really taken the time to notice or appreciate the decorations and surroundings.

The town's usual Christmas

decorations adorned the public areas. Artificial holly wreaths were hanging from each lamp post and corner street sign, and shiny garland was strung between the posts. The Town Hall building had a Christmas tree at the top of the steps, and garland was strung between the columns across the front of the building.

A large banner had been hung above the road in front of the Town Hall building. It had large red and green letters that said, "Little Red Truck Christmas Festival - Welcome!"

The little town was full of people, as it had been the previous two days as well. There were certainly more people milling around than Chuck could ever remember seeing there before. And, there seemed to be even more here today on this last day than there had been on the previous two days.

Chuck had noticed a number of vintage trucks parked throughout the town all weekend. A few of the vendors, and even some guests, had driven their own red trucks into town, and other colors too. Some had been fully and pristenely restored, and others were not. Several even had custom chrome wheels and other non-standard additions. Chuck thought maybe they should include a truck and car show next time if they ever did this again. "I will have to remember to suggest that to Jackie and Susan," he thought to himself.

He found a parking space down a back street from the town square. It was a nice enough day to just walk the rest of the way. He didn't want to park too close to the center of town anyway, in order to allow for more visitors to get closer spaces.

Jackie had said she would meet him in front of the main display this morning. As he approached the town square, he saw that the crowd surrounding their red truck display was just as full as it had been on the previous two days. People were certainly taking full advantage of the photo opportunity it provided.

The display had turned out nicely. It was just as Jackie had first described it to Chuck. Their two trucks were facing each other, and the Christmas tree they had picked out was positioned directly in the center behind them.

It was a very large tree as Jackie had desired. She wanted it to be tall enough to reach almost to the top of the stone wall behind it. When they had returned to the tree farm to pick up the one they had selected, Chuck was afraid it would be too large to fit in his truck, but it did actually fit. And now, with the star on top, it was slightly taller than the wall. Jackie had been pleased when they placed it into position.

Now it stood there, strategically placed in the center of the display, decorated with various assorted ornaments. There were gingerbread men and women, different colored candy canes, spherical globe ornaments of different colors, a Nativity scene and, of course, little red truck ornaments. All of which were large, so they could be seen well and also match the size of the tree.

On the ground, directly in front of the tree, was a stack of gifts. Each was wrapped in colored gift paper, most of which was buffalo check print. That was another idea of Jackie's since buffalo check was so popular.

There was a holly wreath on the door of each of their trucks. Chuck's magnet idea had worked perfectly for attaching them there with no damage to the trucks and no visible hooks or strings. The wreath on Chuck's truck had a blue bow, and the one on Jackie's truck had a purple bow. Jackie had selected those colors as they were each of their favorites.

There was a string of multi-colored Christmas lights hanging across the entire width of the wall. They were shining brightly against the grays and browns of the stones.

When Jackie had first suggested the lights, Chuck questioned how they would be powered. Jackie said she had found a power outlet that was conveniently placed at the end of the wall for use at concerts and other events. She had thought that should work rather well for the lights, and she was right.

People were lined up at the display, patiently waiting for their turn to take photos with the trucks. Some would include only one truck in their shots, and some would try to get back far enough to include both trucks. That was quite difficult with the number of people everywhere, but folks seemed to try to cooperate with each other and even take photos for others. It was quite refreshing to Chuck to see people working so well together for a change.

Everyone seemed to really enjoy seeing the trucks and were having a grand time. A few adults had a challenge keeping their young ones from climbing on the trucks, but they were doing a pretty good job.

"I hope I didn't keep you waiting long." It was Jackie's voice. Chuck turned around to see her walking toward him. Susan was close behind her.

"Good morning," Chuck said as Jackie approached and hugged him gently.

"Good morning to you too!" Jackie replied, and then she kissed his cheek.

"Good morning, you two," Susan said as she joined them. "This weekend has been a huge success. It has been tremendous, actually. Thanks to the two of you, and others of course."

Susan then began to share that the local restaurants have been full every day of the festival, for every meal. The hotels were all booked solid for the whole weekend and even a few days before and after that.

"Thank you two for all you did to pull

this off," Susan continued, "and for encouraging me through it all."

"You are more than welcome," Jackie replied as she hugged Susan.

"Yes, you are very welcome," Chuck added.

"Was it enough to save the town?" Jackie asked. "Or, do you know that yet?"

"It was definitely enough to get things rolling and stimulated," Susan answered. "So, yes, it was enough.

"I was just telling Pastor Randall and Martha a few minutes ago that the main thing is how the local businesses have been affected and responded," Susan continued. "I talked to several of the owners throughout the weekend and they are very encouraged. More than they have been in a long time. A few of them, who had been considering closing and moving to a larger city, are now convinced to stay."

"That is fantastic!" Jackie stated with a huge smile and as she lightly clapped her hands in excitement.

"Many of the business owners hope that we will have this festival every year," Susan continued.

"That would be great!" Jackie said, with an even bigger smile on her face. "My author friend drew a very large crowd this weekend too. He has been selling and signing a lot of books, and he hopes we will do this again and invite him back. All of the vendors have told me the same thing. It has been a huge success for them."

"I have talked to a few of the Town Council members," Susan said. "They agree we should continue this festival as a new tradition for our town."

"That is awesome!" Jackie responded.

Chuck grinned and thought to himself that if any more good news was shared, Jackie was going to explode from the excitement.

Jackie paused in thought and then continued. "I just wish we could have honored

Mr. Miller with the festival in some way.”

“The town was important enough to him to sell everything to help save it all those years ago,” Chuck said, “so, I think that by our efforts to save the town once again we are honoring his wishes.

“Plus,” Chuck added, “we are using his truck to help save the town, so that is also honoring him in a way. His truck was used in his efforts to save the town, and now it is helping to save the town again.”

“Very true,” Jackie acknowledged. “And now, yours is too. I just wish he could see it.”

“That reminds me,” Susan said as she looked around as if searching for someone. “I have a surprise for you. Someone is supposed to meet me here in a moment.”

Susan once again looked around to see if she could locate her expected party.

“Ah, here he comes now,” Susan said as she stepped forward to meet an older gentleman who was approaching them.

"This is Jackie and Chuck that I told you about," Susan said to the man as she turned back toward her two freinds. He extended his hand toward them, and they each shook it. "Jackie and Chuck, this is Mr. Samuel Miller."

Jackie was speechless for a moment. She didn't know what to say.

"Mr. Miller was one of our town's previous mayors," Susan continued with a sly grin and wink toward Jackie.

"Good to meet you, Mr. Miller," Jackie said. "Are you enjoying the festival?"

"I'm enjoying it very much," he answered. "I still keep up with some of your local news now and then, and when I read about your festival, I considered attending. Then, when I got Mayor Wellers' letter, I decided to come for certain."

"Letter?" Jackie asked, somewhat surprised.

"I wrote a letter to all of the previous mayors of our town," Susan explained. "All of the ones that I could, at least. I wanted to let them know about the festival and to invite them to attend."

"And, I am so very glad that you did," Mr. Miller replied. "It has been a real pleasure being back here." He stepped toward Jackie's truck and said, "This truck looks very familiar. I owned one just like it many years ago."

"Mr. Miller," Jackie said. "This is the same truck. This was your truck. My grandfather was the one who bought it from you. He left it to me." She smiled as she paused.

"I found your old registration in the glove box," Jackie added to prevent him from suspecting she knew anything beyond that.

"That's how I know it was yours."

"How wonderful," Mr. Miller replied. "I am so glad to see it found a good home and a good use in your festival too.”

“Yes, Sir,” Jackie replied. “It sure has been of great use.”

“That does my heart good.” Mr. Miller smiled, and then he stepped toward Chuck’s truck. “And, who does this newly restored gem belong to?”

“That is mine, Sir.” Chuck answered. Mr. Miller asked him some questions about it, and Chuck began to share the story of his restoration project. He even shared about the fuel pump being used from Jackie’s truck.

Jackie seized the moment and pulled Susan aside and said quietly, “So, that was the big secret you were working on.”

“Yes,” Susan answered. “Just my way of thanking you for everything you did. I thought it would be a good way to get him here without revealing your secret.”

“It was a great idea,” Jackie said. “Thank you.”

“You’re welcome, my friend,” Susan

replied as she hugged her.

When the two men turned toward them once again, Susan said to Mr. Miller, "Let me introduce you to some other folks in town." She stepped toward him and took his arm. "Please excuse us for a little bit."

"Of course," Jackie responded. "It was so good to meet you, Mr. Miller."

"It was nice to meet you too," he replied. "I hope your festival is a huge success."

"It has been already," Jackie stated. "The Lord has blessed us greatly."

"He is good at doing that," Mr. Miller said with a smile. "You have a great rest of the weekend."

"Thank you. You do the same. And, enjoy the festival."

Jackie then watched as Susan and Mr. Miller walked away and into the crowd.

"You are right," Chuck stated, "the Lord did bless our festival. And, He also blessed your desire to honor Mr. Miller."

Jackie turned back toward him, and Chuck noticed there were tears welling up in her eyes.

"He sure did," Jackie said with a slight emotional break in her voice. "Thank you for all you did to help with this festival, and with helping me to solve my mystery," Jackie said as she took Chuck's hand and held it.

"You are more than welcome," Chuck replied.

He put his arm around her waist and pulled her close. Then, they kissed.

What is *Your* Decision?

Have you decided to accept God's free gift of salvation? Do you know for sure that you are saved and will go to heaven one day? The Bible tells us that we cannot get to heaven on our own.

"For all have sinned and fall short of the glory of God." **Romans 3:23**

We have all sinned, whether it was lying, stealing, sinful thoughts, or other sins. That means we have broken God's Commands - His Rules - His Laws - which means we are sinners and deserve death.

"For the wages of sin is death." **Romans 6:23a**

But, Jesus paid that penalty of death for us.

"But God demonstrates His own love for us in this: While we were still sinners, Christ died for us." **Romans 5:8**

"For God so loved the world that He gave His one and only Son, that whoever believes in Him shall not perish but have eternal life." **John 3:16**

So, if we believe in Jesus, we can have eternal life in heaven. But, what do we need to *believe* about Him?

"For what I received I passed on to you as of first importance: that Christ died for our sins according to the Scriptures, that He was buried, that He was raised on the third day according to the Scriptures." **1 Corinthians 15:3-4**

"If you declare with your mouth, 'Jesus is Lord,' and believe in your heart that God raised Him from the dead, you will be saved." **Romans 10:9**

We need to believe that Jesus died for our sins and rose again from the dead. When we do, we receive God's free gift of salvation.

"The gift of God is eternal life in Christ Jesus our Lord." **Romans 6:23b**

If you wish to receive that free gift of salvation, pray the following prayer:

Lord Jesus, I know that I am a sinner and do not deserve, and cannot earn, eternal life in heaven. I believe You died for my sins and rose from the dead to purchase a place in heaven for me. Lord Jesus, come into my life. Take control of my life. Forgive my sins and save me. I repent of my sins and now place my trust in You for my salvation. I accept your free gift of eternal life. Amen.

If you prayed that prayer and truly meant it, then congratulations - you are saved! You have a place reserved for you in heaven. You are now a part of God's family.

"For, 'Everyone who calls on the name of the Lord will be saved.'" **Romans 10:13**

Here are some suggestions of some things for you to do next:

- Tell someone about your decision to accept Jesus as your Savior.

- Find a local, Bible-believing church to attend.

- Get a Bible and start reading it. A good place to start is in the book of John (the 4th book in the New Testament).

The Lord bless you on your new journey with Him!

Feel free to contact the author at
rick@rhinoprints.net
*or visit him at **facebook.com/RickEllingerBooks***

Other Books by Rick Ellinger

Visit **Facebook.com/RickEllingerBooks**

for more info and more books by this author

Visit **Facebook.com/MyLittleRedTruck**

for magnets, mugs and other home decor items

featuring the little red trucks on the cover of this

book - and other color trucks